For my students,
with respect and gratitude,
and to Jane Bow
and Andrew Wooldridge
—thanks for the chance.

Exposure

Patricia Murdoch

orca soundings

ORCA BOOK PUBLISHERS

FIC
Mur

Library and Archives Canada Cataloguing in Publication

Murdoch, Patricia, 1957-

Exposure / Patricia Murdoch.

(Orca soundings)

ISBN 1-55143-523-3 (bound) ISBN 1-55143-493-8 (pbk.)

I. Title. II. Series.

PS8576.U585E96 2006   jC813'.54   C2006-900406-4

Summary: Julie is presented with a perfect opportunity to get
back at her tormentor.

First published in the United States, 2006
Library of Congress Control Number: 2006921035

Orca Book Publishers gratefully acknowledges the support for its
publishing programs provided by the following agencies: the Government
of Canada through the Book Publishing Industry Development Program
and the Canada Council for the Arts, and the Province of British
Columbia through the BC Arts Council
and the Book Publishing Tax Credit.

Cover design: Lynn O'Rourke
Cover photography: Bigshot Media

Orca Book Publishers   Orca Book Publishers
PO Box 5626 Stn.B   PO Box 468
Victoria, BC Canada   Custer, WA USA
V8R 6S4   98240-0468

www.orcabook.com
Printed and bound in Canada
Printed on 100% PCW paper.
09 08 07 06 • 5 4 3 2

Chapter One

As I came in the front door of the school, I could see Dana and Brynn, their heads close together as they whispered. There was no way I was going to risk walking past them. Dana would say something or bump me or make me drop my books—anything to make me look like a total jerk in front of everyone else.

A hundred kids went up the stairs. I veered right and walked down the main hallway to get to the other stairwell. It took longer, but it gave me a brief moment of peace.

Sammy, my best friend, was attempting to stuff her backpack into the locker we shared.

"There you are, Julie. I didn't see you. I hate this stinking locker," she hissed between the pushing and the kicking.

"I need my math book," I told her.

"You're kidding, right? I just got this in here. Hey, I love your shirt. When did you get it?" She began tugging on her pack to pull it out.

"Yesterday. It feels kind of tight," I told her. I was aware that every bulge and roll was visible.

"It's supposed to. Shows off the good stuff."

I laughed. "Yeah, but it shows all the bad stuff too. Makes me feel weird."

"Get over it," she said with a grin.

"Easy for you to say, you're so thin. How come you never wear tight clothes?" I asked her.

Sammy looked down at her chest. "What you call thin, others call flat as a board, or flat as a boy, as my sister says."

Nothing ever seemed to really get to Sammy. Not that she didn't get mad, but even when she did, she was funny about it.

I noticed Dana coming toward us. I tensed up, right on cue.

"If your fat gut didn't stick out farther than your boobs, your shirt wouldn't look so stupid," she said as she passed me. She didn't slow down, didn't even really look at me. Just dropped her insult and went into the classroom.

"Ignore her," said Sammy. "You look good." She handed me my math book and started cramming her backpack into the locker.

"She's right. I do look fat and stupid. I wish I hadn't worn it." I knew something like this was going to happen. I had looked in the mirror that morning and told myself I looked ridiculous, but I was tired of never being able to wear the same clothes everyone else wore.

"Why do you let her get to you? Who cares what she thinks?" asked Sammy.

"Everyone in this entire school, that's who. Do you have your extra gym shirt here?"

"You let her win every time."

"Do not. I want your shirt."

Sammy sighed. "This is the last time I'm taking this out. Is there anything else you want?"

Mr. Charles stepped out of the room. "Hurry up, girls. The anthem is going to start any moment now."

"Can I go to the washroom? I need to change," I asked him. I held up the sweatshirt as proof.

"If you have to."

"Come with me, Sammy," I pleaded, grabbing her arm.

"You would think that you would be able to go to the washroom by yourself," he said. "Sammy, take your seat."

Sammy crossed her eyes and stuck

out her tongue when he wasn't looking. I grinned, then pretended I was stretching out my neck when he spun around and glared at me.

I hit the bathroom door with both palms; it made me feel like I owned the place. Two younger girls were just finishing their makeup. They were already trying to get in with the seniors. They had probably been successful. One of them was actually fatter than me, but I bet Dana left her alone. I glanced at myself. I'm not really fat, not like those people whose thighs rub together and stomachs hang down. I just don't have a waist. I look like a cylinder.

I pulled the sweatshirt over my head. Sammy always bought really baggy clothes, so they would usually fit me—her shirts would anyway. Never her pants. I felt better immediately. Hidden. Protected. I waited a couple of minutes and then went back to class.

Our first class was English and there was a substitute teacher. Having a substitute was always a change from the routine, and you could almost feel the electricity in the air. It felt a little bit like Christmas. But then we saw who it was. Old Lady Beeton. She'd been a teacher here before she retired and became a substitute. Now she had to prove she still had it. Within five minutes, Josh, the class clown, had been sent to the principal's office. Devon went soon after. Mrs. Beeton was even complaining about some of the girls. It wasn't much fun. At least the class assignment called for group work. I nodded at Sammy as the instructions were read. We would probably team up with Marie and Sara.

"And I will be making the groups," said Mrs. Beeton. "Two names from the top of the list, and two from the bottom. If you don't like your group, then you are welcome to tell the principal all your troubles."

My stomach churned. I'd be in Dana's group. Wasn't it enough that I had to sit in front of her in math? I had thought Charles was the only teacher left on the planet who used alphabetical order, but Beeton seemed pretty pleased with herself. Maybe they lost all humanity as they got older.

I considered my options. I could kick the chair over and get sent to the office, but then I'd be grounded for an eternity and have to spend quality time with Mom. I could fake a stomach ache, or girl problems, and ask to use the phone. By the time they got hold of my mom I could say I was feeling better. But then I'd get the lecture on getting enough sleep and not staying up listening to music.

Dana had already told Ben and Tom, the other two members of our group, where they should sit. I grabbed my books and headed toward them.

"This should be good," she said. "Julie will add that homely, I mean, homey touch to our group."

The boys smiled.

I wished I could hit her, blast her head off, dig things into her eyes. I slumped into the chair. "Whatever."

"Somebody's not happy today?" Dana said sweetly.

I picked at the edge of my binder and didn't look at her.

"All right, class, you should get started brainstorming all the different settings where the novel took place," said Mrs. Beeton. "And then make a list of all the main characters and the problems they dealt with in each setting."

I knew the novel inside out. I had the thing practically memorized. I could have written the whole report. I said nothing.

"Did anyone even read that stupid book?" Dana asked in disgust. "I was much too busy to do any schoolwork."

None of us said anything.

"Well, if you must know, I had to go shopping on Friday, and on Saturday there was a party at…ooops…I'm not supposed to say, but he's in grade twelve."

Like we care, I thought. Just shut up.

"Grade twelve guys are so much better than the losers here," she continued. "A bunch of them were there, and there was just Brynn and me who weren't in their class."

"Some of the groups seem slow to get writing," Beeton commented, a vague threat in her voice.

"I'll get the paper and markers," I said, looking for any excuse to get away from her. I wanted to tell Sammy how much Dana was bragging, but her group was talking and working and actually had stuff written on their paper. I picked the ugliest colors I could find in the plastic basket and yanked the paper off the pad so the corner was ripped.

I plunked them in front of the group and said, "Somebody else is writing."

Beeton was on patrol.

"I'll do it," said Dana in a loud, cheery voice as Beeton came closer.

"I bet you already did it," Ben mumbled.

I laughed before I could stop myself. It must have been loud, because most of the class was staring at me.

"What's so funny, young lady?" Beeton asked.

I would have loved to tell the class what Ben said, but I could feel Dana's cold blue eyes burning at me. "It was nothing," I mumbled.

"Get back to work, and consider that your warning."

"Yes, ma'am." I knew my face was scarlet.

Dana leaned close to me, closer than she had ever been if she weren't pushing me. "If you ever make fun of me again, you fat loser, I will make sure your life is so bad here, you'll regret the day you met me."

That day had arrived years ago.

I closed my eyes and let the darkness block her out. I spent the rest of class digging at the hole I had made in my binder. One day I would get even with her.

Chapter Two

During lunch Sammy and I decided we had to do something about the mess in our locker. It was only the start of October, but it wouldn't be long before we'd have to be cramming winter coats in there as well.

Dana was at her locker, but Brandon was with her, so I knew I was invisible for a while. I wished I could ignore her, but it was like a hangnail. I just couldn't leave it alone. I wished everyone talking and shouting in the hall would shut up so I could hear better.

"Can't you move?" Dana asked him. "I can't see the frigging numbers. You're so lucky you got to sleep in. And you didn't call me last night. This day just sucks."

Brandon glanced our way, as if he could feel me watching, but I acted like I hadn't noticed anything. He shuffled over a few steps to give her more room.

I moved to the other side of the locker so I could watch without having to keep twisting my head around.

"How'd you do at the tournament?" she asked, her voice suddenly soft and babyish.

"We won. Naturally. We'll take the division, and then the playoffs. But I got a couple of five-minute penalties. Real cheap. The ref just had it in for me."

Brandon was really hot, but all he talked about was hockey. Everyone said he might be good enough to play professionally, or at least get a scholarship somewhere. I couldn't figure out why he was with Dana. She wasn't very nice to him. But of course, she was Dana. She got whatever she wanted.

The second bell rang.

"Gotta go," he said.

"Call me?" she asked.

"I'll try, but I have another practice, and we got back later than usual last night. That's why I didn't come over," he called to her as he headed down the hall.

As soon as he was gone, she saw me. "What are you looking at?"

I kept my eyes straight ahead and waited for her to go to class. Kelsey walked by and slipped a note onto Dana's books. Dana must not have noticed, and the note fell. I waited a moment, then picked it up.

"Is that my note?" she hissed at me, her hand stretched out.

I shrugged.

"It says DANA ONLY on it? Can't you read?"

I gave it to her.

"You didn't read this, did you?"

I shook my head.

"You better not have."

She took the note to her desk and I followed a few steps behind.

I hated sitting in front of her. I hated the thought that she was looking at the back of my head. What if I had dandruff or a pimple? There were times when I could feel lasers boring into my skull. I wished I had left the shirt on. I glanced back over my shoulder and saw Dana staring at my armpit, almost in a trance. I turned back and moments later felt something push into the flesh just above my bra strap.

I brushed it away and knocked Dana's pencil to the floor. Had she been poking me?

"Now you did it," she said. "Pick it up."

I leaned down to get it, too surprised to do anything else. My shirt pulled up as I moved forward.

"XL underwear?" she said, loud enough for almost everyone to hear.

I straightened up. My head was pounding. My arms felt as if they weren't attached to my body. I don't know what I did with the pencil. Why was this happening?

Something sharp hit me in the middle of the spine.

"Sorry, my book slipped. Hope it didn't hurt."

I wasn't sure if I was breathing. I didn't know what to do. I couldn't cause a scene. I couldn't tell. I couldn't cry. It would make it worse. My chest tightened and my lungs clawed at the air. I looked to Sammy. She was staring at me with eyes wide open.

Then I heard Dana swear softly as she tore the note into little pieces.

Chapter Three

"So, did anyone say you looked nice in your new shirt?" my mother asked. She was shoveling steaming lasagna onto plates.

I didn't answer. Did she really want to know? I looked at my brother Zack as he shoved an enormous hunk of bread into his mouth.

"Honey?"

What was I supposed to say? Tell her the truth? She'd get all flustered and probably cry. I should just say it was fine, that Sammy said it looked good. But I couldn't. I dove in headfirst. "You just want to say 'I told you so,' don't you? You told me not to wear it."

Her face dropped. "That's not what…"

I couldn't stop. "If you must know, they called me a fat loser. That stupid Dana made fun of me and threatened to make everyone in the school hate me. Are you happy now?" I felt worse. Lashing out at her was too easy. She never stopped you.

"Oh no!" She sat down. "My poor baby. Perhaps she didn't mean it?"

There was no point talking to her. "I just told you she made fun of me. How can someone not mean it?"

"Julie, honey, you're getting angry. Can't you just ignore her?"

"I don't know why I bother telling you anything."

"Well, this is just not acceptable. I'm not going to sit by while someone bullies my child. I'm going to phone the principal."

She wouldn't actually do that, would she? "Don't, Mom, that would just make it worse," I pleaded.

"I want that girl stopped," she said.

If the principal spoke to Dana, my life really would be over. I would have to leave the school. "Please don't, Mom."

"Yeah, Mom, you shouldn't phone the school," my brother said.

I looked at him. He was helping me out. I couldn't believe it.

"Then I'll phone that girl's parents. They should know how mean their daughter is."

It was going from bad to worse.

"That's not too good either," Zack said. "Julie should handle this on her own. It'll blow over in a day or two. They'll find someone else to pick on."

"On someone else's baby. That's not right."

I didn't care about anyone else. All I cared about was not having my mother do something that would mean I had no chance of surviving at school. "I'll stay away from her, Mom, really I will. And I'll ignore her when she makes fun of me, just like you said." I tried to smile, to show her everything was fine.

"I don't like it, but if you're sure, I'll leave it alone. As long as you know I'm here to help you."

"I know you are, Mom." I changed the subject. "This is really good lasagna. Did you do something different?" I could feel the anger slowly retreat back into its hole.

"I did add a new cheese this time. I didn't think anyone would notice."

"Can I have some more?" I asked. I was so hungry. I could eat the whole pan. At least there was lots of fresh, warm bread.

Zack and Mom discussed the school's new policy of banning all backpacks and cell phones. I smiled occasionally and nodded, but I was more interested in my dinner.

After clearing the table, I went to the family room. Zack was plugged into his video games on the old TV, and I had the good one to myself. My favorite show was on. The lead actor was unbelievably good-looking.

"How can you stand this junk?" Zack asked, looking up from his game.

Then the lead female character came in, wearing mostly nothing. Zack came and sat on the couch.

"You can be a real jerk sometimes," I told him. "But you sure helped me with Mom."

He grunted. "I hate the way she gets so worked up. Last year when I got flattened playing football, she made me go to Emergency, even though I told her I was fine. And then she phoned the coach to complain that the game was too rough. I didn't even try out this year."

Mom meant well, but she really had no clue what was going on.

"That girl's name was Dana?" he asked.

"Yeah. So?"

"Is she pretty? Long brown hair?"

"I wouldn't say pretty, but she's got

brown hair. Do you know her?" He had my full attention.

"Not really. But she might have been one of the girlies at Scott's on Saturday night."

"Dana was bragging about some party. Was there a skinny girl named Brynn there? Kind of ugly, with braces?" I asked.

"That's got to be them. What a joke. They were all over Scott. Talking about how much they drink. Everybody was laughing at them."

I could feel the grin spread across my face. "How come they were at the party?"

"I don't know. Somebody knew somebody who thought they'd be possibles. Dana anyway. Brynn was just part of the deal."

The show had gone to commercial and Zack stood up. I wanted to know more; he couldn't stop now. But if I acted desperate, he might figure he had made a mistake telling me that much. "Yeah?" I said, trying to sound casual. "What're *possibles*?"

"You tell anyone and I swear you'll regret it."

Why was everyone always threatening me? "I won't."

"Well, Scott's a real pig. He gets his kicks having girls hang off him." He smiled. "Not that I'd mind that myself, but not the young ones. That's just perverted. It's like he thinks he's some kind of celebrity and they're his groupies."

"Does he...do they...you know?" I wanted to know. "Does he do it with them?" It was disgusting but fascinating at the same time.

Zack shook his head. "He's not that stupid. He could end up in jail if he did. But he likes to do everything but go all the way. Some of the stuff he wants them to do isn't right. Then he dumps them."

I felt as if I was floating, running on air. I had this wonderful, mile-high pile of stuff on Dana. "Does he always dump them?"

Zack nodded. "He doesn't keep them for long. If his girlfriend found out, she'd kill him."

"He has a girlfriend? And he's doing that?" I couldn't believe it. But then again, Dana had Brandon and she'd been there, doing that. I wondered if Scott knew, or cared.

"It's amazing what he gets away with. Always says the girl is somebody else's if she finds out. She's not exactly Einstein."

I couldn't wait to tell Sammy.

"You better not tell anyone," he said. "Got that? Not anyone. If Scott found out where the leak came from, he'd probably have me beaten up."

He looked serious. Around here? People could get other people beaten up? It sounded like TV.

"I probably shouldn't have told you."

"I won't tell, I promise. Really, I won't." I didn't think I would. At least, I'd try not to.

"Not even that wacko friend of yours."

"Sammy's not wacko," I said. Well, maybe some of the time.

"Yeah, right."

"You should talk. You're the one with the sick friends. How come you hang around with Scott anyway?" I asked.

Zack shrugged. "Nothing else to do. Besides, it's entertaining. And sometimes there's extra girls to go around."

I was surprised by that. Zack was mostly just a royal pain in the butt, but I didn't think he'd need anybody's leftovers. I could see that some girls would even think he wasn't totally bad-looking.

"What are you two talking about so intently?" asked Mom, appearing in the doorway unexpectedly.

"Nothing," I answered. She would freak if I told her. It was a little tempting, just to watch her react, but I didn't seriously consider it. She looked hurt enough by my answer as it was.

"Well, you know Zack, Mom, all he can talk about are his stupid video games," I added, feeling guilty.

"You do really need some hobbies, Zack," she said. "Aren't there any girls you're interested in?"

"Mom," he answered in a flat tone.

"All right, I know, out of bounds." She smiled and left the room.

Zack plugged his head back into his earphones and I returned to the show, although it couldn't keep my interest. I was full of the dirt I had on Dana.

Chapter Four

The next morning I felt better about going to school than I had for a long time. When the bell rang I didn't hang back like I normally do. I pushed my way up to Sammy and went up the regular stairs. I could see Dana at the top of the stairs, looking more vicious than usual, half-blocking traffic so everyone would have to look at her as they passed. My shoulder blades started to tighten, waiting to see what she'd do to me. Even though I had an arsenal of information, I was anxious.

She glanced at me and shook her head, then turned back to her little crowd.

It was worse than a comment. She just shook her head as if I was some dead animal on the side of the road that she felt a twinge of pity for. She didn't know what I knew.

"Isn't that new kid's name Scott?" I asked loudly.

"What new kid?" Sammy asked. "What are you talking about?"

I ignored her. I was watching to see if Dana would react to the name. And she did. She spun around and stared at me.

"Yeah, I heard his name was Scott," I repeated.

Dana's eyes narrowed.

"For the second time," said Sammy, "what new kid are you talking about?"

I couldn't believe the rush that went through me. Dana was momentarily in my control. I wanted to squeeze the situation till it dripped Dana.

"Am I invisible here?" Sammy asked. She shoved me. "Earth to Julie, come in. What kid?"

Dana kept staring at me.

I could feel it crumble. "Uh…that guy, he just moved here."

Dana's face immediately went back to flawless. A smile formed at the corners of her mouth. "Hey, if he's new, he might not yet know what a great catch you'd be. Go for it." And she walked toward her locker.

There were snickers.

I had gone from feeling like the queen of the world to a big fat nothing in less than a minute.

"What was that all about?" Sammy asked. "Sometimes you are even weirder than me."

I was too upset to tell her the story just then. I went to the safety of the washroom.

The pair of girls standing by the sink looked at me. I went to a cubicle. The door was out of line with the frame and I couldn't get it to lock. I leaned my back against it.

Dana had won again. It was too much. I kicked the toilet-paper dispenser. The metal front tore loose from one of the screws. It was bent and twisted.

What had I done that for? Whenever I got angry, something bad happened. Someone was going to tell. They always did. I laughed. Sometimes it was me doing the telling.

I had to find a way to get back at her. Just once she should feel like the fool.

The get-to-class music began to play. I gave a little tug on the dispenser and it felt like it would fall off in my hands. I patted it gently, as if it were a puppy that I hoped would do as I asked. I went to class.

"What was with you?" Sammy asked. "And what was Dana so weird about?"

I wondered if I should tell her. Zack had warned me, but I knew it was only a matter of time before I told her. I had never been able to keep anything from her. I had never even wanted to. So the sooner the better. The teacher gave his instructions and retired to his desk. We were supposed to be comparing two books by the same author. Sammy and I had already finished our first book, and we asked if we could go to the library to pick out another. He sighed and nodded. "If you have to…"

We picked out our books and settled into our favorite spot under the make-shift stage. I told her everything. Almost everything. I left out the part about Zack waiting for the leftover girls.

"That is so pathetic, and he's got a girlfriend?"

"And what about Brandon?" I asked.

"You're right. Something's going on with him too. He wasn't at Dana's locker this morning, and Brynn was rushing around talking to everyone. I think it involves Amy."

"This is great. I hope something big happens and Dana is crushed into the ground," I said.

"That's a little harsh, isn't it?"

"You know how she treats me," I said defensively.

"Maybe you could just wish that she left you alone."

Like that would be enough, I thought. But Sammy always wanted things nice and fair. "Yeah, sure," I answered. "That would be good." Time to change the subject. "I wonder if we'll ever have to worry about guys like Scott."

"Somehow I doubt that they'll be after us," she replied.

The truth of her statement took a moment to sink in.

"But it's not because we're losers," she said hurriedly. "They're the losers."

"I'm not so sure," I replied.

Chapter Five

In my next class I ended up sitting beside Sammy, right at the back of the room. We could see everything. Best of all, there was no Dana behind me.

And there was a fight brewing between Amy and Dana. They hadn't said a word to each other, but everyone knew it was on. It seemed as if I had just dropped off Dana's radar screen. Life would be so good if it were like that all the time.

Friday night, Sammy came over to watch a movie.

"I'm picking you up at ten; be ready in the driveway," Sammy said, eyes slightly bugged and her head cricked to one side as she repeated her mother's parting words.

I laughed. "I wish you could sleep over. Zack's out and my mom always goes to bed early. I hate watching TV alone."

"Me too, but Mom says I don't get enough sleep when I stay here, and I've got my dance class at 8:00 tomorrow morning."

I was lucky if Sammy got to stay over more than three or four times a year. There was no point thinking about it. "I got a couple of choices from the movie store." I spread them out on the coffee table.

"Where's Zack?"

I looked at her. "Oh, yuck. You don't like him, do you?"

"No, I just asked. Just showing a neighborly interest in the activities of my friend and her family."

"But it's Zack. That's just sick. You and my brother. And besides, he's too old for you."

"He's only a couple of years older than me," said Sammy. "My dad's ten years older than my mom."

"That's different. And as if your mom would let you out on a date anyway."

"I can date when I'm twenty-five and married."

"You can date when you're married?"

"This is my mother we're talking about."

Sammy left at 10:00 on the dot. Mom went to bed soon after. I returned to the family room and put in a second movie. It was way more fun when Sammy was there.

At 11:00 the back door opened. It was too early for Zack. What if it were a thief? A home invasion? Before I could think about hiding, I heard Zack swear as he tripped over the dog.

"You're still up?" Zack asked, coming into the room. He was obviously annoyed.

"You scared the life out of me!" I said

angrily. "What are you doing home so early?"

"None of your business." He sat on the couch, picked up the remote and changed the channel.

"Hey, I was watching that," I said.

"Like I care?" Zack shot back.

"What are you so crabby about? No leftovers tonight?"

"Shut up!" he said angrily.

I was stung. "I was just asking." I could smell the beer on his breath.

He flicked aimlessly through the channels. "Anything to eat in this place?"

"There's chips. I could get them."

He nodded.

I went to the kitchen. Something wasn't right. Zack was never this stressed. He always let things roll off him. I got a bag of chips out of the cupboard and took two cans of pop from the fridge.

His hands were shaking when he took the drink.

"You all right?" I asked. He didn't say anything. "What happened tonight?"

He answered, staring straight ahead as if he were talking to the TV. "We were out in the forest, back by the sand dunes."

I nodded.

"We had this nice little fire going, playing a few CDs. Lots of people. Cooler of drinks, somebody had a couple of joints. It was pretty cool."

I nibbled at the ridges of my chip.

"Those girlies from your school were there. That Dana sucked back three coolers, one after another." He stopped talking.

He opened the can of pop and pulled the tab off. He flicked it against the wall. "It was pretty mellow. A bunch of them started dancing."

I sipped my pop.

"That Scott, though, man, he's got serious problems. He keeps giving the girls more booze. And he's making whoever comes up for a beer kiss him first. It was funny to begin with, but the girls were getting too drunk. One of them threw up right by the fire. We kicked sand on it, but it still stunk."

I waited while he drank the whole pop at once and then burped. I felt as if I was watching a movie.

"Then Scott gets out a digital camera. Tells me he's got someone in Toronto who will give him $200 for a card with girls on it."

I felt cold and pulled the afghan over me.

"So he starts taking all these pictures…" He paused and rubbed the back of his neck. "They were too gone to know. Couple of them began to take off their shirts. And Scott's just pointing and clicking. He even stopped to erase the pictures that didn't show anything." He took a deep breath.

I waited.

"Then Scott starts wanting the rest of us to get in on it. I was thinking they'd have to be morons to do stuff like that on camera. But they're too stupid to even be morons. So they're kissing, and Scott gets one of the girls to…you don't need to know…I sort of hoped I could just fade out, sneak away when no one was looking. But all of a sudden we hear this guy yelling that the cops are coming. The girls started screaming. Brynn tried to get Dana to put her clothes back on. I took off, then realized I had forgotten my backpack. I went back to get it. The cops were talking to Dana and a couple of other girls who were too drunk to run. They didn't even see me. One of the cruisers was blocking the entrance to the parking lot, but Steve had parked on the side road, so I got a lift with him."

I didn't know what to say. I was glad he was home and the cops hadn't got him. Mostly I was glad Dana got caught.

"You better not tell Mom," he said.

That was the last thing on my mind. "What are you going to do?"

"Nothing." He stood up. "But I'm staying the hell away from Scott." He went upstairs.

I stared at the TV for a few minutes, not watching. There was a lot to think about. I turned off the TV and went to turn off the lamp. I stumbled over Zack's backpack.

If he had any beer in it, Mom would freak. She thought he was such a Goody Two-shoes. I looked in his pack. Under his sweatshirt was a digital camera.

Chapter Six

I slept terribly. I kept waking up. I couldn't tell if I was thinking I was asleep or dreaming I was awake. I could not stop thinking about that camera. I wanted to see what was on it, but our computer was in the living room. The light from the monitor would have shone down the hall. Zack or Mom could easily find out what I was doing. I decided that my only chance was to get up early, before they woke up.

The alarm woke me at 6:00. Zack's backpack hadn't been moved. I took out the camera and popped out the memory card. It looked so small and plain. "Let's see what you've got." I tiptoed to the living room.

With a few clicks of the mouse I had the first image on the screen. The people were hard to see; they were too far away and the flash was too bright. The next one was clearer. Dana was dancing. Her arms were above her head and there were boys staring at her. In the next few photos there were people kissing. I couldn't tell for sure, but one girl looked like Dana. In one of the pictures Zack was sitting with a bunch of the others, beer bottles in their hands.

The pictures were disturbing. I wanted to stop but it was like driving past an accident on the highway. I had to look. Dana was topless. The boys were getting closer. It didn't look romantic like it did on TV. It looked cold and angry.

In one of the final pictures a girl was being pushed toward Zack, and he had his arms open. Not quite the way he told it.

The last picture was of a boy. He had turned the camera around and taken his own picture. The picture was out of focus and the flash lit up the boy's nose, but he was grinning. It had to be Scott.

I removed the card from the computer. I felt sick. The pictures were ugly. Scott was a creep. There were bad pictures of Zack. But...but I had stuff on Dana now, real stuff, and that could change everything.

There were so many things I could do. I could let Dana know I had them, and if she ever bothered me again I'd show them to people, like an insurance plan. Or I could print a few of them and just drop them in the hall at school. Dana would have to change schools. My pulse was pounding in my ears.

Then a deliciously wicked idea came to me. I could get the photos back to Scott to sell them to his person in Toronto, and every pervert in the world could get a glimpse of Dana.

I realized I was biting my nails. I had

tried to break the habit a million times, but couldn't. The ends of my second and third fingers were raw.

Did Zack know the camera was in his backpack? He hadn't said anything last night, but he could have been covering up. If he didn't put the camera there, who did? Was it Scott? If it was, he would definitely want it back. When would he come for it?

I couldn't keep the card. What was I thinking? Zack would know it was missing. But I could make a copy of it.

I heard noises upstairs. The dog was prowling. Every day he waited for Mom to get out of bed before he would leave her bedroom. I listened. No other sounds came from upstairs. I was thankful I hadn't turned the computer off. I burned a CD of the photographs.

I could hear water running in Mom's bathroom. I shoved the camera into the backpack and raced back to the family room. The dog's nails were clicking on the hardwood floor. The disc. I still had to hide it. When Mom was in the kitchen making coffee, I snuck back to my bedroom. Where could I hide it? Mom rarely came in, but sometimes she'd pick up dirty clothes or change the bedding. Where would she never look? Everything looked like it had a reason she might touch it. Except for the great pile of junk on the top of my desk. There was stuff there from last year. I could put the disc right into the middle of it and know it was safe.

"Morning, honey," my mother said.

I gasped.

"Didn't mean to startle you. But I heard you moving around. You're up early."

"Just couldn't sleep. How about you? How did you sleep?"

"I heard Zack come in last night. It was nice he wasn't out late. I worry about him sometimes." She leaned over and kissed my cheek. "I'm glad you don't give me any cause for worry. Can I fix you something special for breakfast?"

"Sure," I answered. "Waffles?"

"Coming up."

She went to the kitchen. I flopped on my bed and stared at the ceiling. I was exhausted and it wasn't even 6:30.

Chapter Seven

Ever since we were little, Zack and I have watched cartoons on Saturday mornings. Back then we'd get up at dawn, but as we got older we slept in longer and longer. This morning I couldn't wait for Zack to wake up on his own. The minutes had been crawling by. At 9:00 I knocked on his door.

"Get lost," came a muffled voice.

"Are you awake?" I asked.

"Are you deaf?" Zack said more loudly. "Get lost."

"I need to talk to you," I said to the door. I slowly turned the handle. "Really, Zack, this is important. I'm coming in."

He was buried under his blankets and pillow. "What?"

"It's about last night...when I was watching TV this morning I accidentally picked up your backpack, and...and a camera fell out."

Zack sat up. "What?"

"Like I said, it was an accident, but a camera fell out. And I know you said last night there was a camera."

"It was in my backpack? Who put it there?"

"How would I know?"

"Let me see it."

"I put it back, it's in the family room."

"Get out so I can get dressed."

I closed the door and went to the family room. Moments later Zack was digging through his pack.

He swore. "I can't have this," he said,

holding it as far from his body as he could.

"I bet Scott will want it back," I said.

"No kidding…"

The phone rang. And rang. I picked it up. It was Sammy.

"Did you hear?" Sammy was so wound up she was shouting into the phone. She nearly blew my ear off.

"About what?" I asked.

"There were cops at Dana's house last night. My mom heard it from Dana's mother's best friend. Dana was attacked or something last night, and now the cops are looking for the guys who did it."

I looked at Zack. "Do they know who they are?"

"I don't think so. Seems like Dana doesn't remember too much, or that's what she's saying. But why would she want to protect someone who attacked her, right? But they've got some other people. Nothing this big has ever happened. This is so exciting! And it serves that Dana right."

"Was she hurt?"

"Don't think so, but my Mom says her parents are calling lawyers and cops and maybe even a private investigator, and they're going to make Dana go to counseling." She took a deep breath. "I wonder who it was. Do you think Zack might know? Ask him, okay?"

I wanted to hang up. Sammy's gossipy tone bugged me. "My mom's yelling at me to clean up after the dog. Let me know if you hear anything else."

"Oh, okay. You know, you're so focused on hating Dana, I thought you'd be happier about this," she said.

"I am, really, it's just that I didn't sleep too well last night. I'll call you this afternoon."

She hung up.

"Who was that?" Zack asked.

"Sammy. Her mom was talking to a friend of Dana's mom, and they've got cops and everything trying to find out who attacked her."

"Nobody touched her. What do you mean, attacked?"

"That's what her mother said."

"Maybe they're trying to make it look like it wasn't her fault. I knew those girlies were no good."

"You've got the camera," I said. "You could prove she was part of it."

Zack swore again.

"What are you going to do with it?" I asked. "Are you going to give it to the cops?"

Zack looked at me as if I was stupid. "Do you know what would happen to me if I did? The trouble everyone would be in?"

"But what if the police find out you were there and they come here and search our house and find the camera?"

"They can't do that. Can they?" he asked.

"I don't know. I think they can do pretty much anything they want. You've got to get rid of it."

"I know."

"You could give it back to Scott," I said.

"Yeah, that's a real good idea. I'll walk

up to him and say, 'Here's the camera you were taking pictures with to sell to some guy and, yeah, that might be a cop car over there watching me give this to you.' They wouldn't need to check for fingerprints. They could just arrest us."

Fingerprints? Mine were all over the camera and the card. I had to wipe them off. "Do you know what's on it?" I asked, trying to sound innocent. I took the camera out of his hand and started wiping it with my sleeve.

He shook his head. "But I can imagine."

"Are you going to look?"

"Why would I? I've got to figure out a way to get rid of it." He paced.

I was a little afraid of him.

"Maybe I can take it back to the forest and hide it," he said. "Then if Scott asks me where it is, I'll tell him I don't know, I never had it. Yeah, that's a good plan. Give it to me."

I had to think fast. My fingerprints were on the card, inside the camera, and maybe I wouldn't be able to get them all off. And

51

Zack was in some of the pictures. I wanted to tell him to at least delete those ones, but then he'd know I lied. I should have erased the card after I made the copy. Maybe the cops had a way to get at the pictures even after they'd been erased, like they were still there somewhere. There's always talk about not being able to really erase stuff on your hard drive.

What was I going to do?

Zack was staring at me as if I was out of my mind. "Give it back to me."

I didn't want to let it go. If I had a new card, one I hadn't touched with my bare hands, then it would be okay. When they found it and saw it was blank, maybe they'd think something had messed up and the camera hadn't worked.

"Your plan is good, Zack," I said. "But I think I have an even better one." I explained about putting in a blank card in case there were incriminating pictures of him. He seemed to get the logic. "And if you go back to the forest, the cops might see you and wonder what you're doing there. I could go for a bike ride with Sammy, like we're just goofing around, and I could drop it. We could pretend like we don't know anything."

Zack scratched his head. "Yeah, maybe that would be better. I'd sure owe you one."

"More like a billion," I said.

Chapter Eight

I stopped in at the camera store in the little mall on my way to Sammy's. It took almost all of Zack's money, but I bought a card. I put on the thin winter gloves I'd brought, took out the old card and put the new one in. I put the original in the holder and tucked it into my pocket. I should have just thrown it out with the packaging, but I couldn't.

"You were so weird on the phone,"

complained Sammy when she opened the door. "What's going on?"

"I am swearing you to complete secrecy. You can never tell another person, promise?"

"Sure. What is it?" she said.

"I mean it, you can't tell." I was starting to sound like Zack.

"All right, I promise."

I told her about the camera and the party. I had thought I would tell her everything, but I changed my mind. There was something in her "I'm better than everyone else" attitude that was getting on my nerves. She'd disapprove of Zack, and she'd really hate that I burned the CD and kept the pictures. It was best that she think we were getting rid of it all.

"Well, if we have to go that far, I'm taking something to eat," Sammy said. "You want something?"

We filled Sammy's pack with drinks and snacks.

"What if we get stopped by the police?" Sammy asked.

"We can just say we're out biking around. The food helps."

The ride was long, but the cool weather made it more comfortable. It was fun until we got near the conservation area. I began to imagine that the place would be swarming with police cars.

The parking lot was empty.

We followed the dirt road to the dunes. No one was around.

It was clear from the bottles and garbage and picnic tables that we were in the right place. In some areas the wind had blown the sand smooth, but in other areas there were many footprints.

What was it like last night? There would have been music and voices. It was silent now, just as it had been in the photographs: Dana, doing those things, but with the sound turned off. I almost felt sorry for her. "We need to ditch this somewhere close, but not too close."

We leaned our bikes against a picnic table.

"How about there?" Sammy suggested,

pointing at a small pile of branches and leaves. It was a few feet off the road. A pack could have easily fallen and ended up there.

"Looks okay. I just want to get rid of it."

We lifted up the branches and placed the pack on the ground. I kicked at the dirt a few times and then put the branches on top. "Add a few more leaves."

Sammy shook her head. "We don't want it to look like it's been here for days. It'll look phony."

She was right.

I removed one of the branches. Now it looked more like it had just fallen. "Let's get out of here," she said nervously.

"I'm hungry," I said. "I want to eat." I also wanted to stick around for a bit and see if anything happened.

"Me too, but not right here. Let's go back to the parking lot."

We rode back. There were no picnic tables, so we sat on the wood-rail fence.

"I never asked you, did you see the pictures?" asked Sammy.

I wanted to tell her, to share the secret, but I wasn't sure if I should.

"You did, didn't you! I can tell by how long it took you to answer. Tell me what was on it."

I gave in. I described most of the shots, but left out the fact that there were photos of Zack. Especially if she did have a crush on him. I didn't like that idea much, but I didn't want her to think he was a pervert.

"Did she look all gross and drunk?" she asked.

"Yeah, it was pretty sad," I said. "And the guys were disgusting."

"Did it show her getting attacked?"

"She wasn't attacked, at least not in the pictures, and Zack said the cops came before anything happened."

"That is so like her," Sammy said angrily. "Gets into trouble and has to make it all huge and the worst thing ever. I can't wait to tell everyone she was just drunk and being a loser."

I grabbed her arm. "You can't tell anyone anything! You promised! And if you did, then someone would think you saw the pictures, and you could get in trouble with the police."

"I forgot. Sorry. What good is having such a juicy bit of information if you can't tell anyone? This sucks."

"You promised. You don't want that Scott guy after you, do you?"

"Him? No." She shivered. "If I forget again, just remind me about him."

A police cruiser crept slowly into the parking lot.

"Oh-oh," I said.

"Act normal, eat something," said Sammy.

The officer got out of his car. He came over to us and smiled. "Nice day for a picnic, isn't it, ladies?"

"Yes, sir," I answered.

"Have you seen much going on this morning?" he asked, picking up a stone and throwing it into the bush.

"No, sir."

"No cars or dirt bikes or people hanging around?"

"No, sir," I replied again. "Just Sammy and me, getting some exercise."

Sammy stuffed the last of her brownie into her mouth and nodded in agreement.

"Do you mind telling me your names?" He took out a pad and pen.

"Are we in trouble?" I asked. The memory card felt like it was the size of a CD in my pocket.

He smiled again. "No, no, this is just routine," he said. "We are looking into a bush party that happened here last night. Did you girls hear anything about it?"

We didn't dare look at each other.

"Uh, no," I said.

"Me either," added Sammy.

We told him our names and addresses. My mother would have a fit if he called.

"If you do see anything unusual you could give me a call, or the crime reporting unit. You can get money for tips," he said. "And you never have to give your name." He put the pad away. He looked around a little more and then, leaving his cruiser in the parking lot, headed down the road we had just come back on.

"Let's get out of here," Sammy hissed.

"Wait a minute. We've got to act like we're not scared to death."

We waited till he was out of sight, then put on our packs and rode away as fast as we could.

When I got in the door, Zack stood up so quickly he tipped his chair over backward.

"What took you so long?" he demanded.

"It's a long way by bike, and we got tired. We took a couple of breaks."

"Did you get rid of it?"

"Uh-huh," I said. "There was a cop there too, but we didn't tell him anything."

"I hope you didn't. Mom took a phone call for me. The message said Scott had phoned and he would call back later."

I got a drink of water. The phone rang.

"Talk about timing," I said. "You better pick it up before Mom does."

Zack grabbed the phone.

I could only hear his side of the conversation. Zack did a lot of listening and a lot of denying. No, he didn't have his backpack, must have left it in the forest. No, he didn't have the camera. No, he didn't see who might have taken it. No, he hadn't gotten any phone calls from anyone. Yes, he understood. Yes, he got the big picture. Yes, he realized how much was at stake. Yes, he knew Scott had connections.

"Did he threaten you?" I asked when he had hung up.

"Not really, sort of, indirectly."

"Maybe we should call the police."

"And say what?" he said. "That you returned the pack and lied to the officer earlier? That would go over well."

I sighed. It had quickly become a bigger problem than I had thought.

"You did put in the blank card, didn't you?" he asked.

"I said I did."

"What about the original?"

"I'll get rid of it," I said.

"Give it to me. I've got to make sure it's destroyed."

I handed him the plastic holder.

He took out the card and tried to snap it, but failed. "I'm going to smash it with a hammer." He went downstairs to the basement.

He pounded so many times there could only have been dust left.

Chapter Nine

During English class on Monday morning, Sammy and I got permission to go to the library again. Once the teachers think you like to read, they always let you go. Hardly a day went by when we didn't spend twenty minutes talking on the cushions tucked under the makeshift drama stage. The librarian didn't seem to care as long as we were quiet.

We heard raised voices in the hall.

"What do you mean you won't tell us who they are?" said a man.

"Mr. Manning, your voice is very loud and classes are in session," our principal, Mrs. Kent, answered. "Perhaps we can talk in my office?"

It was Dana's father! No wonder he was upset.

"We're not going anywhere until you give us some information."

"Could we at least step into the library, and out of the hall?" Mrs. Kent said.

We heard several people enter the library. They were very close to us. Sammy and I stared at each other. They didn't know we were there. It was too good to be true.

"Now, Mr. and Mrs. Manning, I'm not sure why you think I have any more information than you do."

"Our daughter said a girl who used to go to this school talked her into going to a party, and there were boys there who spiked her pop," said Mr. Manning more quietly.

I desperately wanted to talk to Sammy, but all we could do was bug our eyes at each other. My foot had fallen asleep under me, but I was too afraid to move it in case they heard us.

"I understand that you must be very upset," said Mrs. Kent in a soothing tone. "I have heard something of the events of the weekend, but, trust me, I do not have any more information than you have."

"Our daughter says you have pictures of every student, past and present, and I want her to look through them so I can find out who this girl is and where she lives."

"I'm afraid I can't allow you to do that. Student information is confidential."

"What is that supposed to mean?" said Mr. Manning. "My daughter's been taken advantage of and you don't care?"

There was silence. Sammy tried to peer through the stage stairs and bumped her head. We froze. No one seemed to have heard.

"Well, we're certainly glad that Dana

has recovered enough to return to school so soon after such a traumatic incident."

The principal's voice hadn't changed. Was she being sarcastic, or did she mean it? I got the impression that she maybe didn't completely believe Dana's story. Man, this was good. Maybe Dana wouldn't be the precious little girl anymore. All the students knew what a controlling, nasty person she was, but the teachers never seemed to figure it out. They all thought she was sweet and smart and perfect.

"I'm phoning the school board then," Mr. Manning said, his voice rising. "You can't get away with talking to me like that. I'll have your job so fast you won't know up from down."

"I'll have the secretary give you the number."

"I can't believe I'm not getting any help. An innocent girl is attacked and no one even cares. Not the cops, not the school."

"I'm sure the police will get to the truth," the principal said.

"I hope so," I whispered softly, crossing my fingers.

"Let's go, dear," Mrs. Manning said. "Thank you for your time."

"Good luck," said the principal. "Are you sure you're up to going to class, Dana?"

Dana was there?

"And you remember," her father said, "no phone, no TV, no computer and straight home after school."

"But, Daddy…"

The door closed and the library was silent again.

"That was too cool," Sammy said. "I'd like to have heard what she told her dad."

"And he believed her!" How could he not know what his daughter was like? "We better get out of here."

"Not too soon," warned Sammy. "Or someone might see us."

We were becoming masters of the unnoticed exit.

"If he believed her," Sammy said, "I wonder why she's so grounded?"

She had a point. But moments later a class came in for their library time and we didn't talk about it again.

I was happier than I had been for a long time. Everything was crashing down around Dana. Finally I was getting some justice. But I wanted a bigger helping. This wasn't enough. I had to do something.

I went into the washroom and dug a marker out of my pencil case. I drew a box and a couple of circles, with lines for a flash going off, on the outer wall of the first cubicle. No one would be able to miss it. It didn't look exactly like a camera, but it would do. And for the finishing touch I wrote SMILE DANA, with a happy face right beside it.

Chapter Ten

Each time someone left the classroom, I hoped they would discover my message, but it took until almost recess. Then it fell into place. Kelsey got Brynn, who got Dana. They ignored the teacher's commands to return to their desks.

At break there was a fight. An actual fight. Dana grabbed Amy's jacket and yanked on it so hard she fell. Amy got back up and kicked Dana right in the stomach.

They screamed at each other. Dana called her the most obscene words I had ever heard, and Amy told Dana she was crazy. I noticed Brandon stayed back when everyone else started running over to watch.

The teachers finally separated the two girls and escorted them to the office.

Dana blamed Amy! I hadn't even considered that possibility. The camera had been smudged out, so most of the students didn't know what had really started the fight. They figured it was because Amy stole Brandon.

For once Dana looked bad. It was all right to fight the usual way—trashing your enemy, spreading rumors—but it wasn't okay to fight like the boys. It made you look too rough. My mother said they used to call girls like that tomboys. It's not what they were called now.

If I could keep putting things out there and cause this much trouble, my life would be heaven. I avoided Sammy. If she heard it was a camera, she would know it was me. Who else could it have been?

She would think I was mean. She could be such a child sometimes.

Dana and Amy were sent home. Sammy was in agreement with everyone else that Brandon was at the heart of the fight. Life was sweet.

But by the end of the day the talk had gained a new tone. Amy deserved what she got. Dana only did what any other girl would do in the same circumstance but was too afraid to. Dana was a wild child. Dana was hanging out with grade twelve boys. Dana was hotter than ever.

It wasn't supposed to work this way. She couldn't possibly come out on top. But she did.

After school, I went straight home. No one was there. I loaded the disc, scrolled through the pictures and found the one I wanted. A teaser. It was clear who it was, but there was just a hint of what was going on. Just enough to make someone want to see the next picture. I hit Print.

I stood in the doorway while the printer

turned the blank sheet into an object of incredible power. All those tiny splashes of color, nothing by themselves, joined together to create something that could cause so much to happen. I was a little afraid to touch it at first, but I slid it into an envelope and took it to my room.

Zack came home. He looked tired.

He told me that Scott got a buddy to go back to the park, and he found the camera the cops had amazingly overlooked, and it had been blank.

"You don't sound too happy about it," I said.

Zack shook his head. "Scott was suspicious. He said the camera had never messed up like that before, and the battery had been working because he'd seen the flashes. He was glad to have it back, but he said he had a bad feeling."

My mind couldn't settle on Scott, as interesting as it was. I was too focused on the fight. I told Zack about it, but he didn't seem too interested. I realized then that I might have made a huge mistake. I had been extremely lucky Dana blamed Amy. She must have figured Amy had heard about the party from someone. But what if she figured out it really wasn't Amy who did it, and what if she told Scott about the drawing? And what if they thought it was more than just gossip and someone really knew more, and that same person knew about the blank camera that shouldn't be blank? My mind was out of control, racing from one idea to another. Maybe they'd match up a list of people at the party and Dana's enemies, and they'd figure out about Zack and me.

"What were they fighting about?" he asked.

"Brandon."

"I hope she won," he said.

"You do? Why?"

"Well, Scott sure isn't going to be seen with her again," said Zack. "He's thinking of going to live with his dad for the rest of the semester."

"Yes!" I said.

He looked at me and shook his head.

The next morning Dana's mother was in the school office with her. Amy's parents were waiting on the bench in the front hall, but Amy had not come to school. Kids kept making excuses to leave the room so they could cruise by and see if they could find out any details.

At the next break, Sammy and I turned the corner at the bottom of the stairs and almost collided with Dana. She was leaning against the wall, staring at the ground. Her shoulders were hunched, her hair was pulled back in a ponytail, and she didn't have any makeup on.

I felt a twinge of pity for her.

"Are you okay?" Sammy asked her.

Dana paused for a moment. She almost smiled at Sammy; then she looked at me. Her face tightened with anger and she stood up straight.

"You know, no matter what happens in my life, it's still better than yours. If I were you, I'd kill myself."

I was too stunned to move. The violence of her words ripped my chest open. But a funny thing happened. I didn't panic. Instead, my brain slowed. Things were clear. I felt like a huge stone figure from the time of the ancient Greek monsters. My arms were strong, my hands were huge.

I would use the photograph. I would expose her.

Chapter Eleven

I had to decide where to put the photograph. I could e-mail it to everyone I knew, or find some way to post it on a website, but I was pretty sure people would know it was me who'd done it. This had to be anonymous. No one could see me, and it had to be found by students. A teacher might just throw it out or give it to the principal. The girls' bathroom was a logical choice, but there was so much traffic in and out that someone would surely be able to say they had seen me. It had to be somewhere no one would suspect I would go. The library was out. The gym. I hated gym, and we had gym after lunch. The girls' change room. It was ideal. And I would be able to watch Dana's reaction. It was deserted if it wasn't class time. I could enter from the hall and exit through the gym so no one would know where I had been.

I had to wait till lunch.

I made an excuse to get away from Sammy, saying I had to look in the lost and found for my missing gym shoes. The lost and found was just around the corner from the gym. The big bins were filled with filthy clothes, and I wouldn't dream of putting my hand in there, but I stood for a moment, looking down, in case anyone went by. All was quiet. I slipped around the corner and entered the change room. I unfolded the picture and put it on the bench.

I listened at the door that led to the gym and heard voices. I needed to go back the way I had come. If someone was there I would grab the picture and find somewhere else to leave it. The hall was clear. I hurried back to the lost and found bins, pretended to look for another second and then headed outside.

My armpits were soaked. I could feel a trickle of sweat run into my bra. I smelled a little sour. Small price to pay for revenge. I hoped Sammy still had her extra shirt with her.

The photograph had been discovered by the time I arrived in the change room for class. A couple of girls were crushed against the wall, looking at something, their backs turned to the rest of us as we piled into the room.

Dana and Brynn arrived soon after. The girls stared at them.

"You might want to see this," one of them said.

"Is it a naked man?" asked Brynn.

"Not a naked man…" came the answer, and the girls laughed.

Dana took the picture. Her face went white.

Brynn looked at it. "Oh my god."

Dana crumpled the page and ran out of the room.

"You better not tell anyone about this," Brynn threatened us before following her.

"What was it?" Sammy asked the girls.

"Dana had no shirt on. Looks like a party or something."

Sammy glared at me.

I hoped she wouldn't accuse me right then and there.

"I always knew she was like that," said one girl. The comments began to fly.

Sammy grabbed my arm and pulled me into the hall. Her fingers dug into the space between the muscle and the bone.

"You're hurting me!"

"I can't believe you did that!" she hissed.

"She deserved it. You heard what she said to me yesterday. What was I supposed to do?"

"You told me you got rid of the pictures," Sammy said.

"I know." I looked at her sheepishly.

Sammy finally let go of my arm. She looked like she was going to cry. "What's with you?"

"With me? What about her?"

"And now you're the exact same." She sounded sad.

She was right, I knew it. But it didn't really matter. This felt better. "You don't understand."

"Oh, I understand all right," Sammy said angrily. "And I don't like it. I don't like you. I thought you were my best friend, but now I see that I don't really know you at all."

"It's the same me," I protested.

"You were always pathetic?" she asked.

"No…maybe, maybe yes. Maybe we all are, deep down. You just pretend you're not. You just pretend you're better than me."

I didn't recognize the expression on her face. She looked like someone else.

"I…" She stopped herself from finishing her sentence. "I better get out of here."

She was leaving me. "Sammy…"

"Leave me alone for a while. I've got to think about this."

"But, Sammy," I called.

She didn't even look back.

The gym teacher opened the door a crack and hollered for us to get into the gym. He asked about the missing girls but accepted the answer that they were talking to the guidance counselor.

I was surprised to find Dana in the next class. I figured she'd have gone home. But I guess she couldn't really show her parents the picture with that big smile on her face and the drink in her hand after she'd claimed she'd been a victim.

She was sitting with her forehead resting on her books. She didn't even lift her head when the teacher began discussing the causes of the First World War.

The teacher let her be.

About ten minutes into class he put on a video. The sight of the young men waving goodbye to their girlfriends and families was touching, knowing how it would turn out for them. Someone in the class coughed, but it didn't sound like a regular cough. It sounded forced. Then there was another and another. And there was no mistaking it. At the end of each cough was the word *slut*. I couldn't believe the teacher didn't notice, but he was at his desk, marking papers.

Dana heard. She raised her head and looked around. I looked away so she wouldn't catch me watching her. I heard her chair scrape against the floor and saw her walk past. She clasped her hand over her mouth and began to run. She cleared the doorway, then vomited. It splashed on the floor.

Squeals and groans sounded around me. I felt my own stomach heave, but all that came up was a sour taste of bile.

The teacher stopped the video and buzzed the office for a janitor.

My mouth tasted terrible. I asked to be excused. I got a drink of water and watched the janitor as he turned at the top of the stairs.

I went into the bathroom.

"Brynn?" I heard a voice call.

Dana was there, washing her face in the sink.

"Oh, it's you. Get out," she said.

Chunks of food were forming a plug in the drain.

I took one step back, then changed my mind. "You look really gross."

She put her hands on the edge of the sink, as if she needed them for balance. "How dare you talk to me like…" She didn't finish her sentence. Instead she smiled. "It was you, wasn't it?"

I shrugged.

"It makes sense now. That day you were talking about some imaginary Scott. Brynn telling me that someone had seen you in here before that drawing was found."

I smiled. "So, how does it feel to be the loser?" I had waited years to say that to her. I could barely stand how good it felt. Here it was, after all this time.

"You should know."

"Now, that would usually hurt, Dana, but you see, it's this way now. You can't hurt me anymore. I know way too much about you, and I can make your life a living hell. Actually, the way I see it, if I were you, I'd kill myself." There. Justice had been delivered.

Revenge was mine. I was free.

Dana wiped her face with the paper towel, spat in the sink and brushed her wet hair from her eyes. "That's exactly what I'm going to do. Are you happy now?"

Chapter Twelve

I was stunned. I backed out of the washroom and returned to my desk, stepping past the janitor as he cleaned the floor. Dana was going to kill herself? It couldn't be true. People who said it never did it, right? She was just saying that because she wanted me to feel sorry for her, not because she meant it. Knowing Dana, she'd probably go on a rampage through the school, killing everyone else, but not herself. Dana would probably start with me. I tried to get Sammy's eye, but she was still acting as if I didn't exist.

Dana didn't come back. Somebody said she was in the guidance counselor's office again. I didn't know what to do. Should I tell someone? Dana was probably telling the counselor herself, now, so I didn't need to worry.

Sammy disappeared after class and I went looking for her. I had to tell her about Dana. Sammy would know what to do. I finally found her at the far end of the schoolyard, whipping pinecones across the fence.

She didn't even look at me; she just kept gathering up the cones and flinging them at the trees.

"Sammy, please listen to me, something bad has happened."

"You don't say?" Her tone was sharp.

"I saw Dana in the bathroom before she took off."

"Just had to rub it in?"

"But…no, that's not what I…"

"I thought you were better than that."

"I know, but…"

Sammy stopped, pinecone in her hand. "I don't want to hear a word you've got to say. I don't want to hang around with you. I don't even want to know you." She raised her fist with the pinecone in it. Her arm shook. She looked at her hand and let the pinecone drop. "Now I believe it, you are a loser." She ran toward the school.

I watched her go. Sammy had been my best friend. Only friend. Why had I let my hatred of Dana be stronger than my friendship with Sammy? I had made such an incredible mess of things.

My feet started taking me toward the school. I wished and wished I could take it back, that I could undo the damage I had done.

When I got to my locker, all of Sammy's things were gone. She had cleared out. I wanted to cry, but my eyes were dry and my throat was tight. Maybe Mom could help. I could tell her and she would know what to do. Or maybe she'd be like Sammy and realize how horrible I truly was.

I counted the number of cement blocks on the sidewalk on my way home. I couldn't tell Zack either. He would know I had lied and he would kill me. And there was a good chance he'd hear about it anyway; news like this traveled fast. He'd be so angry. And Scott would find out. Who knows what would happen then?

I unlocked the door and dropped my pack on the bench. No one was home. I flicked on the TV, but there were either talk shows or children's programming on. An overweight couple fought and swore and brought out the people they'd been cheating with. That would be me in ten years, I thought. And I'll be the one getting cheated on. I turned it off.

I went to my room and picked up the disc. The late afternoon sun glinted on the gold plastic. The edge felt sharp. I had to get rid of it for real now. But that wasn't enough. Dana had to know it was gone, that there wouldn't be any more pictures.

I would give the disc to Dana.

I immediately felt better. Having a plan was good. I was still scared, but it was the right thing to do. Give the disc to Dana, then Dana will know there's nothing more to be afraid of. The kids will still ride her for a while, but then someone else will do something and Dana will be in the clear. No one will be hurt. All will be forgotten.

I checked Dana's address in the phone book, got my bike out of the garage and headed over. It felt good, not like before. Being mean had felt big and huge, but it was hard inside.

Fifteen minutes later I was at Dana's house. She should have made it home by now. There were no cars in the driveway. I leaned my bike against the railing and stepped up to the front door. I rang the bell. No one came to the door. A few moments later I rang the bell again. Still no one. I looked in through the tall narrow side pane, cupping my hands to reduce the glare. There was a silhouette in the kitchen. It looked like Dana. I pounded on the door. The figure stopped.

"It's Julie!" I shouted at the glass.

Finally the door opened. Dana peered out.

"Can I talk to you? Please?" I said.

"I was sort of busy."

"Just for a minute, please, Dana. It's important. It's about the pictures."

"Oh." She opened the door wider.

I stepped inside.

Chapter Thirteen

Dana closed the door behind me. "What do you want?" She didn't look surprised to see me. Or angry for that matter. Her face was flat, with no expression at all.

"I came to give you the pictures." I offered her the disc.

Dana didn't take it. I thought she'd grab it right out of my hands. She walked away.

"This is all of them, and there aren't any prints," I said.

Dana nodded but did nothing.

"Could we talk a bit?" I asked.

"I don't really want to."

"Please?"

"If you must. Come on."

I followed her into the kitchen. It was like something out of a magazine or a home makeover show. "This is huge. My whole house would fit in your living room."

"Mm."

More silence. I was very uncomfortable. "Can I have a glass of water?" I walked toward the sink. Dana quickly stepped in front of me.

"Uh, how about pop? I'll get you one. You could go in the living room."

"That'd be good."

She didn't move from the sink. "Go sit down."

I had planned to wait for her, but obviously she wanted me gone. I glanced back as I left the room and saw her spread a dishtowel over something in the sink.

A moment later she handed me a can of pop. The coldness felt good on my hands. I scanned the room. "It sure is nice here."

"Where did you get the pictures, anyway? I'd heard there was something wrong with the camera. At least that's what Scott told someone to tell me, I guess. Figures he'd be lying."

"It's a long story, and I don't want other people to get in trouble."

"Like I'd blab that all over the world?"

She was probably right, but I couldn't tell on my brother. "Do you think he heard about the picture?"

"It's not likely. And he's gone, so even if he did, who cares? I hate him."

"Do you think he would hurt me?" I asked, knowing I sounded like a complete baby.

She raised one eyebrow. "Hurt you? Scott? He's all talk. Even after I protected him from the cops he told me never to contact him again. I was so stupid."

"Zack said Scott had friends who would beat him up if he said anything," I said.

"Zack?" she asked.

I couldn't believe I had said that.

"Zack's your brother? Why didn't I figure that out?" Dana said. "Of course. That's how you got the photographs."

"Are you going to tell?" I asked.

She smiled. "No, I'm not going to tell. Who would I tell? And why? There is no way for this to get better."

I was surprised she thought that way. I thought it was already a lot better. She couldn't be thinking about killing herself still, could she?

"Why are you giving this to me?" she asked. "After how horrible I've been to you?"

It was a good question. Why was I doing this? "I don't really know, Dana, but all I know is that it was all too much for me. When I was trying to hurt you, I loved it. But it only lasted for a few seconds. I felt so big and full that I thought I was going to explode."

"You get used to it. The more you do it, the easier it gets."

"It did feel kind of good, like I was…

well, like I was you. But then I couldn't do it anymore."

"I can't do it anymore either," she replied.

The dullness descended again. It started at the top of her head and pulled every muscle down with it. I got scared.

"Here." I put the disc on the table. "Are you okay?"

"Why do you care?"

"I don't know. Just do. But…" I hesitated. I had to ask her. "I've always wanted to know, how come you were so mean to me?"

"I'm not sure, to be honest," she said. "I remember thinking you were a sucky baby and kind of fat, and it just made me angry. And I guess I liked making you cry. And then I just kept doing it."

"That's all? Because I'm not skinny and it was a habit? You made me feel like garbage because of that?"

Dana shrugged. "I really wish there was some deep dark reason, but there isn't. It's just something I do."

I believed her. "I guess there's some good in that," I said. "Maybe I was just in the wrong place at the wrong time. It wasn't my fault."

"Well, it sort of was," she said. "You never did anything, you just took it. Sometimes you'd cry. But you never got angry and that would make me even angrier."

"I was afraid of you, and I was always taught that getting angry was bad. Like you were out of control," I said.

"That's almost funny. All we do in this house is get angry." She laughed to herself. "And you weren't the only one. I've got lots of people who are afraid of me. Maybe everyone."

Her face looked alive again. I could feel my chest loosen.

"Since we're talking, weird as that is, let me ask you something. How could you stand it? How could you go to school?" Dana asked.

"There were days I couldn't go, I would pretend to be sick. And some days

I would just hide from you. But I was not by myself. I had Sammy. And she wasn't afraid of you." Why was that? Why didn't Sammy get caught up in all of it? And now that was in the past. Sammy didn't want to be my friend anymore. "I ruined that."

"I don't think I could handle it," replied Dana. "I can't be by myself. I have to have friends."

"Seriously? I thought you could handle anything. You always look so tough."

Dana smiled. "I wanted it to look that way."

"What are you going to do?" I asked.

"I'm not sure. I don't think I can show my face at school. And my e-mail's full of horrible letters."

"I'm sorry for you."

Dana looked at me.

"And I'm sorry for what I did," I added.

"I don't know if you're going to get this," she said. "I only sort of get it myself, but I'm relieved. It's all busted open. Now it's me. If it didn't feel so bad, it would feel good."

"You're not going to do anything, are you?" I asked.

"Like something stupid? Why stop now?"

My anxiety level skyrocketed. "There's people you can phone. They gave us that number in health class, remember?"

We sang the Kids Help Phone jingle and laughed.

"When does your mom get home?" I asked.

"It might be therapy night, I'm not sure."

"Can I stay till she gets here?"

"To watch me?"

"A little."

"Suit yourself. Want to watch TV?"

We watched a game show in silence. But it didn't feel awkward. It felt warm.

Dana's mother arrived. "Hey, sweetie, how'd your day go?" she called from the kitchen. "I picked up some groceries.

Can you give me a hand putting them away?"

"I'm going to go now," I said.

"DANA! What's this in the sink! DANA!" her mother yelled.

Dana rushed to the kitchen. "I didn't do anything, Mom, it's okay."

Her mother hugged her. "It's not okay. I've got to call the doctor. Something's terribly wrong."

I knew that Dana's mother didn't know I was there until I stepped into the kitchen.

"Who are you?"

"Nobody. I was just waiting with Dana till you got home."

"Did you put her up to this?" she asked.

"Oh, for God's sake, Mom," Dana yelled. "I did it. I collected the bottles. They're my pills. Actually they are your pills. From your bathroom. Julie stopped me from making a really huge mistake. Do you get it, Mom? It's me! I'm the one! It's me."

Her mother pulled her into a tight hug. "I'm sorry," she said to me. "Thanks for staying here. Are you a friend from school?"

Dana looked back at me.

"No. Well, not exactly. And I've got to get going."

"Bye, Julie," Dana whispered.

"Bye, Dana."

The bike ride home passed in a blur. My muscles knew what to do, and I drifted along with them. The autumn air was cool on my face.

Sammy was sitting on my porch. "Your mom said I could wait if I wanted to."

"I was at Dana's. I gave her the disc. Do you still hate me?"

"You're my best friend."

"Thanks."

"Is Dana all right?"

"I hope so."

"Your mom said I could stay for supper too. Lasagna."

The weight was easing away, slipping

from my shoulders. "Are you going to sit next to Zack?"

"Oh good, one little comment and teased forever. Will he be here?"

I laughed. Sammy was an amazing friend. All that bad stuff had been forgiven in an instant.

More Orca Soundings

Crush
by Carrie Mac

Isn't she fazed by any of this? Does she do this all the time? Make unsuspecting, seemingly straight girls squirm? Or am I making it all up? But making up what? The butterflies are real. The fact that I want to kiss her is real.

Would kissing a girl be different from kissing boys? If all I did was kiss her, would that make me queer? Are you queer just for thinking it? Or does doing it make you queer? And what if I don't want to be queer? Do I get a say in this at all?

Because of a moment of indiscretion, Hope's parents send her to New York to spend the summer with her sister. Miserable, Hope ends up meeting Nat and developing a powerful crush. The only problem is that Nat is a girl. Hope is pretty sure she isn't gay. Or is she? Struggling with new feelings, fitting in and a strange city far from home, Hope finds that love—and acceptance—comes in many different forms.

More Orca Soundings

Stuffed
by Eric Walters

"So, do we have a deal?" Mr. Evans asked.

"Unbelievable," I muttered under my breath.

"I don't understand," Mr. Evans said.

"The whole thing is unbelievable. First you try to threaten me. Then you try to bribe me. And now you do the two together, trying to bribe me and threatening me if I don't take the bribe."

"I don't like to think of it in those terms," he said.

When Ian and his classmates watch a documentary about the health concerns of eating fast food, Ian decides to start a boycott against a multinational food chain. Can Ian stand up for what he believes in? Can he take on a corporate behemoth and win?

Exit Point
by Laura Langston

"I'm not dead. I'm still me. I still have a body and everything."

"You are still you, but you don't have a body. What you're seeing is a thought form." He points to a tall gold urn up by the minister. "Your body is in there. You were cremated."

Thunk thunk, thunk thunk. My heart pounds in my chest. Dread mushrooms in my stomach. Sweat beads on my forehead. "But everybody knows death is the end. That there's nothing left but matter."

"Death is only the beginning, Logan. Hannah knows that. Lots of people do."

Logan always takes the easy way out. After a night of drinking and driving, he wakes up to find he has been involved in a car accident and is dead. With the help of his guide, Wade, and the spirit of his grandmother, he realizes he has taken the wrong exit. He wasn't meant to die. His life had a purpose—to save his sister!

Page 1

Tweeg

Oh! Is it morning already?

L.B.

Good morning, Tweed...

Tweeg

You're right, L.B. This could be a good morning. This could be the kind of day that makes ya want to be mean and nasty.

L.B.

You mean like every other day, Tweep?

Tweeg

Yes, but the name is Tweeg. Now, what kind of mischief can I get into today?

Grubby

Gosh, Teddy, why would anyone think about bein' mean and nasty...on purpose?

Teddy

I don't know, Grubby, but Tweeg always does.

Tweeg

Yes, L.B., I'm sure I can think of something to do that will make someone else feel miserable.

Teddy

Well, it was just another normal day for Tweeg...until he looked at himself in the mirror.

Tweeg

EGADS! Look at me, L.B.! What's happened to me? I-I'm raspberry colored with blue spots!

L.B.

Golly, you're right. Them are really pretty colors, too. How did ya do that, Tweef?

Tweeg

I didn't do it. It must have happened during the night. Something's wrong with me!

Grubby

…in more ways than one!

Teddy

Somehow…something happened to Tweeg to make him change colors.

Tweeg

I'm raspberry colored with blue spots! And I can't wash it off! Something's wrong with me! I'm supposed to be green!

L.B.

Maybe you're sick, Tweez. Maybe you've got da…tweezles!

Tweeg

The TWEEZLES?! Oh no, not the tweezles!

L.B.

How do ya feel, Trig?

Tweeg

Feel? I think I feel a little weak…yes, and I-I think I have a fever, yes…my face hurts…my head hurts…oh no, my whole body hurts!

Grubby
What are the tweezles, Teddy?

Teddy
I don't know, Grubby. I've never heard
of them before.

Tweeg
I think I'm going to faint.

L.B.
Maybe you oughta lie down.

Tweeg
You're right, L.B. I should be in bed.

Teddy
So Tweeg went to bed, feeling very bad.

Tweeg
I feel awful. How long do the tweezles
last, L.B.?

L.B.
I don't know.

Tweeg
Are they ever fatal?

L.B.
Are they what?

Tweeg
They must be. No one could survive
feeling this bad. L.B., you've got to do
something to help me.

L.B.
I don't know what to do to help.

Tweeg
Then go out and find someone who does!

L.B.
Okay, Wheeze.

Tweeg

The name is Tweeg.

Teddy

So, Tweeg sent L.B. out to get someone to help him.

Grubby

Yeah, and guess where L.B. decided to go for help...to Newton Gimmick's.

Gimmick

Now the linear fraction disc fits into the matter confuser...and the...

L.B.

Hey, Gimmick.

Gimmick

Huh? Oh my goodness, there's a horrid little Bounder walking right up on my porch...oh, Teddy...Grubby!

Grubby

Yeah, Gimmick?

Teddy

Yes?

Gimmick

Look, fellas. That horrid little Bounder has walked right up on my porch.

Grubby

Gosh! What do ya want, horrid little Bounder?

Teddy

Isn't that L.B.?

L.B.

Yeah, it's L.B., and I'm here to get ya to help Tweeg.

Grubby

Why would we wanna help Tweeg?

L.B.

'Cause he's sick.

Gimmick

Tweeg is sick?

L.B.

Yeah, he has the tweezles.

Gimmick

Then you need a doctor.

L.B.

But der are no doctors around here.

Gimmick

Oh, yes, that's right.

Teddy

Then I think we should try to help him.

Grubby

But why would we wanna help Tweeg?

Teddy

Because Tweeg is Gimmick's neighbor... and helping him would be the neighborly thing to do.

"Be A Good Neighbor"

A neighbor lives right in your
   neighborhood
Whether you like it or not.
What if he shoots cannonballs at you?
Then you'd better hope he is a lousy shot,
Because neighbors aren't likely to just
   go away.

You might be neighbors permanently.
And since a neighbor's someone you see
   every day,
Learn to be neighborly!

Chorus

Be a good neighbor, a really good neighbor
Someday you may be in need.
A little neighborliness
Can help you out of a mess.
It's a cure for loneliness.
It'll bring happiness!
After all, what are good neighbors for?
Ya prob'ly have a neighbor livin' right
   next door!

Appreciate your neighborhood.
You could even start a good neighbor's
  league.
When you help your neighbors it makes
  you feel good.
Even if your neighbor is Tweeg?

Repeat Chorus

A neighbor lives right in your
  neighborhood.
Neighbors are good to spy on.
Not quite, L.B., I think you missed
  the point.

A neighbor should be someone to rely on.
When you go away a neighbor could collect
  your mail.
It's someone who can keep your extra key.
You mean a neighbor could feed my cat
  when I'm in jail?
Learn to be neighborly!

Repeat Chorus

Teddy

So L.B. led us up to Tweeg's tower to see what we could do to help. When we got there, Tweeg looked very, very sick.

Tweeg

I'm so sick. L.B., did you bring someone to help me?

L.B.

Yep, I sure did, Boss. I brought Gimmick and his friends.

Tweeg

What?! Why did you bring those guys?

L.B.

Der de only ones I could think of.

Tweeg
But, but, but, but those goody two shoes...

Grubby
...goody eight shoes!

Gimmick
Alright then, we'll leave.

Tweeg
No, no, no, no, no, stay here. Nothing is worse than being sick. L.B., make sure they don't look at my buttermilk gold formula, alright?

Teddy
We'll try to help, but I'm not sure we know what to do.

Grubby

Well, I know exactly what Tweeg needs.

Teddy

You do?

Tweeg

Ya do?

Grubby

That's right. It's the special Octopede cure for whatever's ailin' ya.

Teddy

What's that?

Grubby

Boiled root soup…it never fails!

Teddy

Really?

Grubby

Absolutely! And I'll even do the cookin'. We'll need some milk…

L.B.

How about buttermilk?

Grubby

Yeah, that'll work…and some spices…

L.B.

Yup.

Grubby

…and a big pot…

L.B.

Right here.

Grubby

…and four pounds of roots.

Teddy

What kind of roots?

Grubby

Them little lavender ones that grow in the sand.

L.B.

We ain't got none of those. I'll have to go out an' dig some up.

Tweeg

Alright, but hurry. I don't know how much longer I can last.

Teddy

After L.B. brought back the roots, Grubby prepared the soup. He cut up the roots and boiled them in the buttermilk, all the while adding spices.

Grubby

Oh boy! Doesn't that smell delicious?

Teddy

Yeah.

Grubby

Alright, here you are, Tweeg. This'll fix ya right up.

Teddy

Grubby started to feed the soup to Tweeg. Tweeg spit the soup out.

Grubby

Hey, what's the matter?

Tweeg

I was wrong. There is something worse than being sick…and it's eating that stuff! Yuck!

Teddy

Well, Tweeg wouldn't eat the root soup. Now what'll we do?

Gimmick

I have an idea!

Teddy

You do?

Gimmick

Yes. It's an old home remedy called a mustard plaster. L.B., do you have any mustard?

L.B.

Yeah, I think so.

Teddy

Gimmick started mixing up a concoction of mustard, horseradish and pepper.

Grubby

Well, if Tweeg didn't like my root soup, I know he won't like this stuff.

Gimmick

No, this isn't to eat.

Tweeg

Ohhh…

L.B.

Don't worry, Tweeg, you'll be alright.

Tweeg

TWEEG?! Well, at least I lived long enough to hear L.B. get my name right.

Gimmick

Alright, Tweeg, let me spread this medication on your chest.

Grubby

We also found out that people can convince themselves that they're sick.

Teddy

That's right. Tweeg wasn't really sick. It was all in his head. It's kind of like how someone who really is sick can start to feel better...with a good attitude.

"A Healthy Attitude"

(Reprise)

A healthy attitude gives you the power
To change your mood from bad to good.
Have a healthy attitude and within
    the hour,
I know that you'll be filled with gratitude.
Have a heaping helping of a healthy
    attitude,
Healthy attitude!

Tweeg

I feel terrific! Now, you goody two-shoes, get outa' here!

Grubby

...goody eight shoes.

Teddy

But we only came here to help.

Tweeg

I said get out of here! Now!

Grubby

You're welcome, Tweeg.

Gimmick

No gratitude!

Tweeg

OUT!

Teddy

Well, I think that was a day we will always remember.

Grubby

Ya can say that again.

Teddy

We learned that a doctor is the only one who should tell people what to do when they're sick.

"A Healthy Attitude"

If the way you feel depends on the
  weather,
The way you look, what you eat, or
  your mood,
Then the world will look a whole lot better
When you have a healthy attitude!
Oh, your attitude's the way you feel
  about things,
And it affects the things you say or do.
Oh, a healthy attitude will make you
  shout things
Like hip-hooray! Boy, oh boy! And
  whoop-dee-doo!

Chorus

A healthy attitude gives you the power
To change your mood from bad to good.
Have a healthy attitude and within
  the hour,
I know that you'll be filled with gratitude,
Because you'll have a healthy attitude!

Now when I look into the mirror,
I see the same old Tweeg I've always seen.
Your complexion is getting so much
  clearer!
Soon I'll be a healthy shade of green!
A healthy attitude will always bring out
The color in your cheeks, a healthy glow.
A healthy attitude will make you sing out,
Do re mi fa so la ti do!

Repeat Chorus

You can convince yourself that you
  have gotten
A rare disease that is making you
  feel rotten.
But now I know it really was a trick.
Yeah, Tweeze, you even make yourself
  sick!

Repeat Chorus

Tweeg

But-but L.B. said I have the tweezles.

L.B.

I said maybe you have the tweezles.

Gimmick

What are the tweezles?

L.B.

I don't know.

Tweeg

You mean you just made it up?

Teddy

Excuse me.

L.B.

Well, I...

Tweeg

You idiot, I haven't been sick at all.

L.B.

Well, you told me you were.

Tweeg

Well, you told me I looked sick.

L.B.

Well, you didn't have to believe me, Tweep

Teddy

Excuse me. I think you made yourself sick
Tweeg.

Teddy

It explains why you turned raspberry colored with blue spots. It's because you drank water from Rainbow Falls.

Tweeg

What?!

Grubby

Yeah, the water made ya change colors. You're not sick at all, Tweeg.

Teddy

Were you drinking this water yesterday, Tweeg?

Tweeg

Yes, but what does...

Gimmick

Then that explains it!

Tweeg & L.B.

Explains what?

Teddy

Grubby dumped the water on Tweeg.
Gimmick, I think that stuff was too
strong.

Gimmick

Yes, you might be right, Teddy.

Grubby

Hey, Teddy, did ya notice the color of
that water?

Teddy

Uh huh! It was orange, and red and
blue...Oh!...Tweeg, where did you get
that water?

Teddy

Gimmick smeared the stuff on Tweeg's chest.

Gimmick

Now this will start to get nice and warm on your chest and make you feel better.

Tweeg

Well, it is getting warm…yes, very warm. It's getting hot. Not just hot, it's burning! I'm on fire! Hey, get it off of me! Get it off!

Teddy

We all hurried to wipe the stuff off Tweeg's chest.

Tweeg

It's still burning!!

Grubby

Let's put some water on him.

L.B.

Here's a bucket of water.